Let's blaaaze!

Blaze and AJ discover Axle City, where
the Monster Machines live!

The Monster Machine World Championship race
is happening today!

Blaze wishes he could race on a track like that.

Bump Bumperman announces that the race will begin soon!

Gabby is the mechanic for the Monster Machines.

Gabby takes Blaze and AJ to meet
the Monster Machine racers.

Stripes is a tiger truck. He's great at leaping and climbing!

Starla is cowgirl truck. No one twirls a lasso like she does!

Darington is a stunt truck who loves doing tricks.

Zeg is a dinosaur truck who loves to smash and bash.

Crusher thinks he's the best racer ever. He will do anything to win—even cheat.

Pickle follows Crusher everywhere.

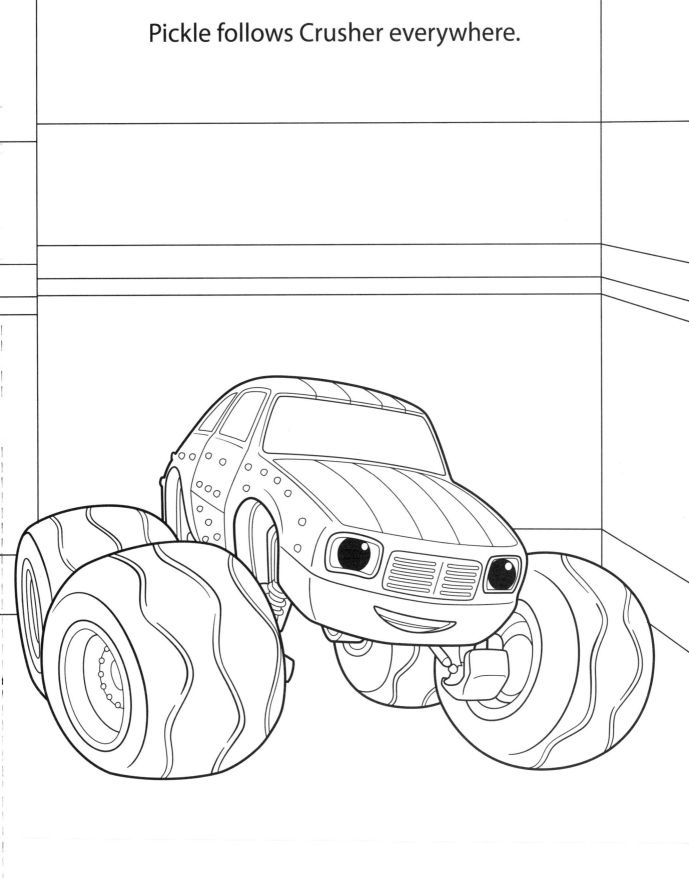

Crusher wants to be the only truck in the race so he can win. He blows bubbles with his Trouble Bubble Wand.

The bubbles pick up the Monster Machines
and carry them away!

Lug nuts! Blaze and AJ are trapped in a bubble!

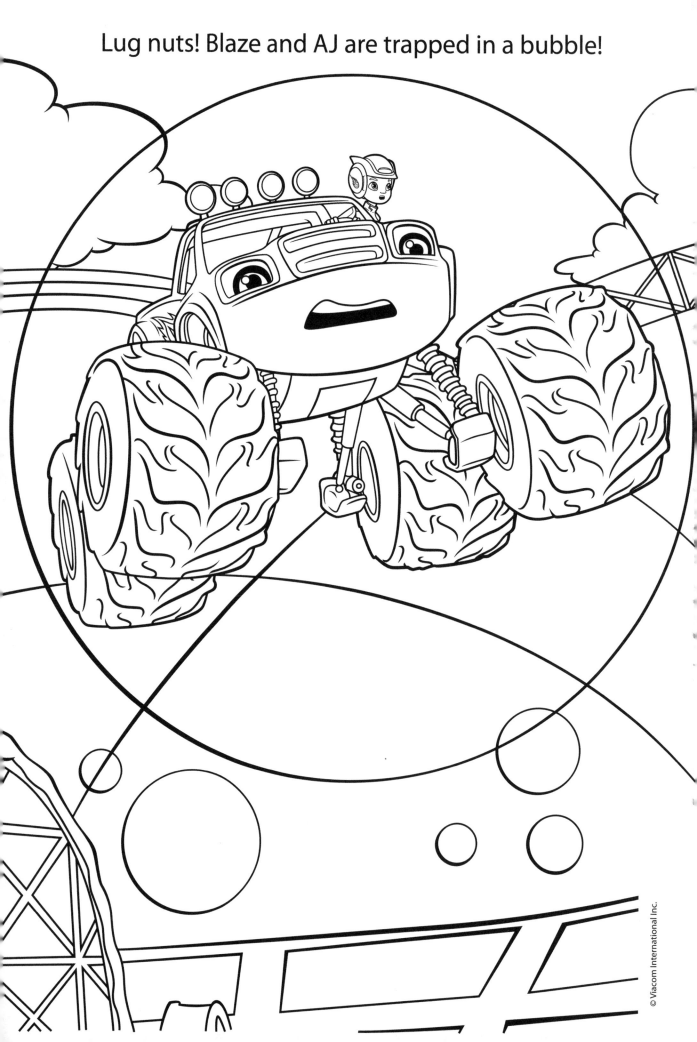

The bubble pops!

Blaze and AJ land in the Badlands.

They see Stripes hanging off a cliff!

AJ turns on his Visor View to find
a way to get to Stripes.

Blaze and AJ jump off a ramp.

Blaze saves Stripes!

Blaze and Stripes zoom back to the Monster Dome before the race starts.

In the forest, Stripes picks up the scent of another Monster Machine.

Darington is hiding from some Grizzly Trucks.

The flat piece of wood and the rock sink, but the curved piece of wood has tall sides to keep the water out!

Safe and dry, everyone floats across.

Back at the Monster Dome,
the crowd cheers!

Crusher doesn't want the other racers to come back.
He builds another device to cheat with.

It's a Mechanical Mudslinger!

The Mechanical Mudslinger flings mud balls
at the Monster Machines!

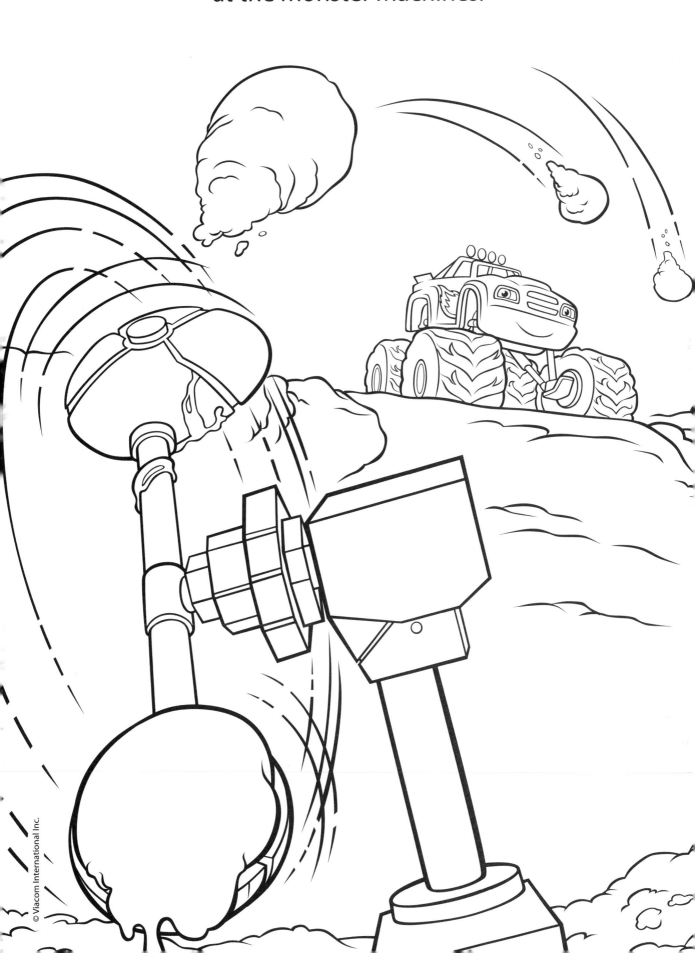

AJ has an idea. With a hose, a nozzle, and a spring-loaded arm, Blaze transforms into a . . .

... water-shooting Monster Machine!

Blaze blasts the mud balls!

Take that, Mechanical Mudslinger!

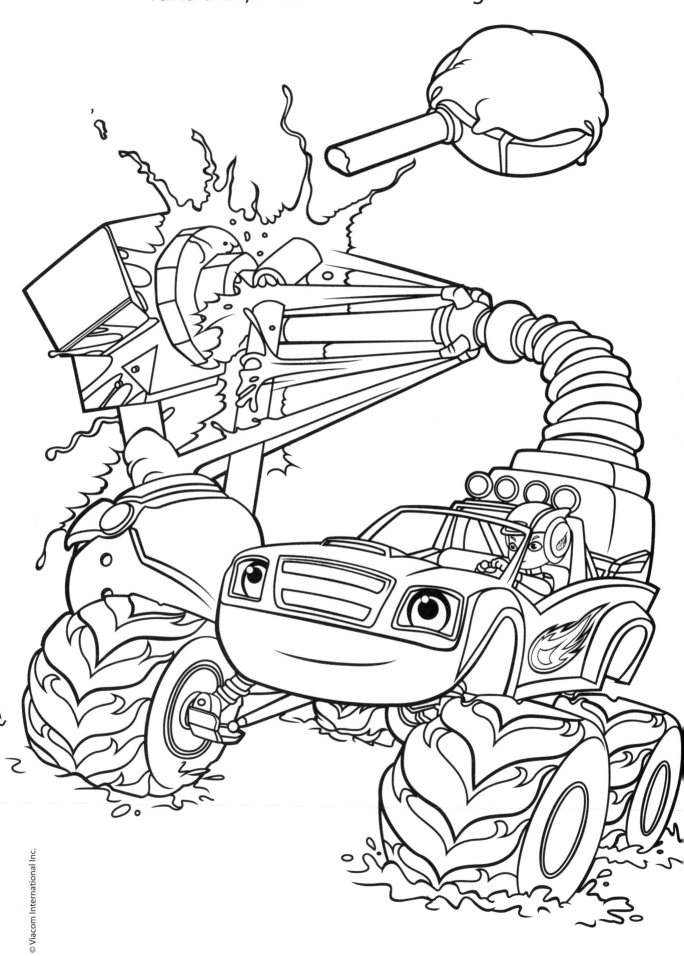

On their way back to the race, the Monster Machines find Zeg rolling down a snowy mountain toward a cliff!

Blaze to the rescue!

The Monster Machines have to go through a cave.
But the entrance is too small!

ZEEEGGGG!

In the cave, they find Starla stuck at the bottom of a hole!

The Monster Machines use a pulley to get her out!

The Monster Machines race back to the Monster Dome together.

Crusher has one trick up his tire—
Robot Knights!

The Robot Knights get power from their shields.

Blaze and AJ use a magnet to take away the Robot Knights' shields—and their power!

The championship race is about to start!
The Monster Machines ask Blaze
to race, too!

On your marks, get set, GO!

Crusher takes
the lead.

Crusher has more
dirty tricks!

Tire trouble!

Crusher's cheating ways are working!

Now it's just Blaze and Crusher.

Using Blazing Speed, Blaze zooms past Crusher!

The winner of the Monster Machine
World Championship is . . . Blaze!